# PRAISE FOR
## THE JASMINE TOGUCHI SERIES

THREE JUNIOR LIBRARY GUILD SELECTIONS

FOUR CHICAGO PUBLIC LIBRARY'S BEST OF THE BEST BOOKS

AN AMAZON.COM BEST CHILDREN'S BOOK

TWO NERDY BOOK CLUB AWARDS

AN EVANSTON PUBLIC LIBRARY'S 101 GREAT BOOKS FOR KIDS

A BANK STREET BEST CHILDREN'S BOOK OF THE YEAR

AN AMELIA BLOOMER LIST TITLE

A CBCC CHOICES LIST (BEST OF THE YEAR)

A BEVERLY CLEARY CHILDREN'S CHOICE AWARD NOMINEE

A 2021 NUTMEG BOOK AWARD NOMINEE

A ROMPER'S 100 PROGRESSIVE BOOKS FOR CHILDREN

A CYBILS AWARD WINNER

A MARYLAND BLUE CRAB YOUNG READER AWARD WINNER FOR TRANSITIONAL FICTION

"In this new early chapter book series, Florence introduces readers to a bright character who is grappling with respecting authority while also forging her own path. Vuković's illustrations are expressive and imbue Jasmine and the Toguchi family with sweetness . . . This first entry nicely balances humor with the challenges of growing up; readers will devour it."
— *School Library Journal* on *Jasmine Toguchi, Mochi Queen*

"Adorable and heartwarming."
— *Booklist* on *Jasmine Toguchi, Mochi Queen*

## ENJOY MORE ADVENTURES WiTH
# JASMINE TOGUCHI

# JASMINE TOGUCHI
## BRAVE EXPLORER

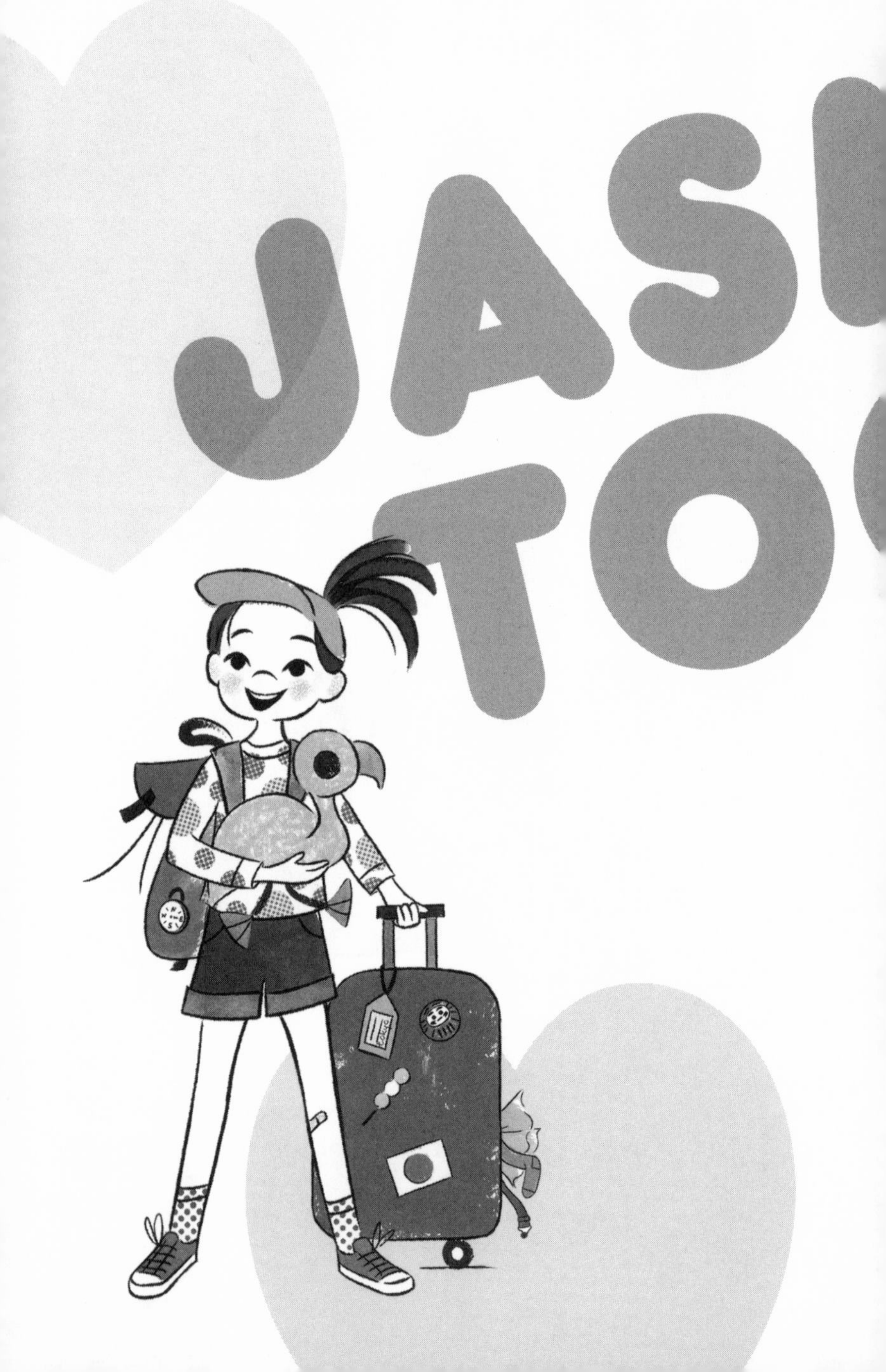

# MINE-GUCHI

## BRAVE EXPLORER

**DEBBI MICHIKO FLORENCE**  PICTURES BY ELIZABET VUKOVIĆ

FARRAR STRAUS GIROUX • NEW YORK

Farrar Straus Giroux Books for Young Readers
An imprint of Macmillan Publishing Group, LLC
120 Broadway, New York, NY 10271 • mackids.com

Our books may be purchased for promotional, educational, or business use.
Please contact your local bookseller or the Macmillan Corporate and Premium
Sales Department at (800) 221-7945 ext. 5442 or by email at
MacmillanSpecialMarkets@macmillan.com.

Library of Congress Cataloging-in-Publication Data
Names: Florence, Debbi Michiko, author. | Vuković, Elizabet, illustrator.
Title: Jasmine Toguchi, brave explorer / Debbi Michiko Florence ; pictures by
    Elizabet Vuković.
Description: First edition. | New York : Farrar Straus Giroux Books for Young
    Readers, 2022. | Series: Jasmine Toguchi ; book 5 | Audience: Ages 6–9. | Summary:
    Eight-year-old Jasmine is enthusiastic about her family's vacation to Japan, but
    once in Tokyo she is distracted by her older sister's grumpiness and her own
    blunders—will she be able to cheer up her sister while finding her own footing?
    Includes author's note and recipe.
Identifiers: LCCN 2022006550 | ISBN 9780374389321 (hardcover)
Subjects: CYAC: Vacations—Fiction. | Sisters—Fiction. | Japanese Americans—
    Fiction. | Tokyo (Japan)—Fiction. | Japan—Fiction. | LCGFT: Novels.
Classification: LCC PZ7.1.F593 Jab 2022 | DDC [Fic]—dc23
LC record available at https://lccn.loc.gov/2022006550

First edition, 2022
Book design by Angela Jun
Printed in the United States of America by Lakeside Book Company,
Crawfordsville, Indiana

10   9   8   7   6   5   4   3   2   1

FOR ALL THE READERS WHO
ASKED FOR MORE JASMINE
TOGUCHI BOOKS —D.M.F.

FOR THE READERS,
THANK YOU! ♡
—E.V.

# CONTENTS

# JASMINE TOGUCHI
## BRAVE EXPLORER

# PACKiNg

Glue stick? Check!

Folder of cutout magazine pictures? Got them!

Felicia the Flamingo? Totally!

Snacks? Yum!

"Whoa! Mom's going to be annoyed with you!"

I turned from the piles on my bed to face my big sister, Sophie. She stood in the doorway of my room.

"Why? I'm doing exactly what she told me to do. I'm packing!" I said proudly.

I, Jasmine Toguchi, love summer. Summer is fun because every day feels like a holiday. But this summer was very special. I was going on a big family vacation. For the first time ever, I was going to Japan. I was excited to have a big adventure!

"It looks like you're making a huge mess." Sophie left to go to the living room or the kitchen or wherever she was headed.

Sophie was two years older than me. She thought that made her smarter than me. This was her first big vacation, too. She was not an expert on packing.

I went back to sorting all the things I would be bringing with me on vacation.

"Jasmine Toguchi! What are you doing?" Mom stepped into my room. She had the wrinkle on her forehead that she gets when she is annoyed.

"Hi, Mom!"

"You're supposed to be packing," she said.

Sometimes parents are not very observant. "I am!"

"What happened to the list I made for you?" Mom asked.

I pointed to my desk. "Over there?" I did not remember for sure where I had put it.

Jasmine's List

☐ TOOTHBRUSH
☐ COMB
☐ UNDERWEAR
☐ PAJAMAS
☐ ONE PERSONAL ITEM

Mom shuffled through my books and papers and markers and pencils. She found her list buried underneath them. "You haven't checked anything off of my list."

"I know," I said. I held up a piece of paper. "I made my own packing list. See? And I've checked off almost everything."

"Jasmine Toguchi," Mom said. She took my list from me. "Remember we had a special family meeting? We talked about how important it was going to be to follow all the rules to make this a fun vacation."

Of course I remembered! It was only yesterday. But I didn't know why she called it a *special meeting*. Mom always had rules for everything.

"Please use my list for packing," she said. She put my list on my desk and handed me her list instead. "I'll be back to check on you."

*Walnuts!* Mom's packing list was boring. It had things like a toothbrush, a comb, underwear, pajamas, and only *one* personal item. There was no way I could pick just one thing of mine to take.

"Told you," Sophie said, poking her head into my room. "I'm packed and ready to leave tomorrow. I can't wait to visit Obaachan and see all the cool places in Japan."

"Same!" I said. "We are going to have a big adventure!"

Sophie actually smiled at me. That made me happy. When she started fifth grade last year, she turned bossy and was not very nice to me. But now she was getting ready to start middle school. For the first time, we would be going to different schools. She would probably miss me. Maybe she would like me again. Maybe this vacation would make us friends again. That would be super-great!

"Seriously," Sophie said, frowning at me. "Get packing. Don't ruin anything by annoying Mom."

Okay, well, maybe Sophie wouldn't be friendly to me right away. I could work on it.

"Mom won't be annoyed with me," I said to my sister, but Sophie was gone.

Then the doorbell rang.

# A IS FOR ADVENTURE!

"I'll get it!" I shouted, and ran to the front door. I knew it was Linnie Green, my very best friend. I was so happy she was here!

I swung open the door. "Hello, Mrs. Green," I said to Linnie's mom. Then I hugged Linnie.

Mom greeted Mrs. Green and invited her in. Mrs. Green was going to stop by our house every day for the two weeks we'd be in Japan. She was going to water the plants and make sure everything in the house was okay. Linnie

would be coming over, too. She was going to take care of my pet fish.

Sophie gave me the fish as a surprise. It was a surprise for sure because Sophie acted like she didn't like me most of the time. But remembering the gift gave me hope that maybe things were changing. Maybe Sophie and I could be friends again.

"I wish you could come with me to Japan," I said to Linnie as we walked into my room.

"Me too." Linnie's eyes got big as she looked around. "Wow. Your room is very messy."

"I know, right?" I said, smiling at her. "I am

trying to decide what things to pack for my trip. I made a list."

Linnie sat on the very corner of my bed. It was the only spot not taken up by piles of my things. Her mouth moved as she read my list silently.

Our third-grade teacher, Ms. Sanchez, taught us how to make lists for good planning. I loved writing lists!

I hopped twice on one foot and three times on the other. I like to jump and hop when I am excited because I have a lot of energy.

"I hope you have room for one more thing," Linnie said when she finished reading.

I peered over her shoulder at my list. "Did I forget something?" I asked.

"I brought you a present," Linnie said.

"You did?" I smiled so big my cheeks hurt.

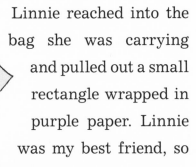

Linnie reached into the bag she was carrying and pulled out a small rectangle wrapped in purple paper. Linnie was my best friend, so she knew that purple was my favorite color, just like I knew green was hers.

I sat on the floor between a pile of flamingo stickers and a stack of books. I slowly peeled off the tape and unwrapped the gift. I like to savor surprises. As the paper fell away, I gasped. It was a purple book! And on the front in gold letters were the words *Jasmine's Journal.*

"Wowee zowee, Linnie! My very own book." I hugged it, and then hugged her. "Thank you!"

"This way you can write down everything you see and do so you can remember it for always," Linnie said.

"That's a great idea, Linnie. I will write down all my great adventures," I said. "And I will share the book with you when I get back."

"I can't wait to read it," Linnie said, smiling. Then her eyes got very sad and her mouth twitched down. "I am really going to miss you, Jasmine."

"Same." Two weeks was a long time. We had never been apart that long before. "But I will talk to you in this book, so it will be almost like we are together."

She looked happy again. I would miss Linnie for sure, but I was super-excited about our vacation. This trip to Japan was going to be an adventure with a capital *A*.

## Jasmine's Journal

Dear Linnie,

I am going to write you letters in this journal so I can tell you all about my vacation in Japan. I have not had any adventures yet unless you count the adventure of packing. It was not much of an adventure though. Mom is only letting me and Sophie bring One Personal Item. It is too hard to pick only one thing.

List of special things I want to take with me:

- Travel Journal—very important because it is a gift from you.

- Felicia Flamingo—Mom said no because Felicia is as tall as me and too big to carry around (says Mom).

- Collage Supplies—Mom said an envelope of magazine pictures, glue stick, scissors, cardboard, and construction paper were too many things and would make a mess (says Mom).

- Daruma, My Fish—Mom said no pets and he would be happier at home anyway (says Mom).

Oh! Guess what? After dinner, Sophie convinced Mom to let us bring *three* personal items! Here is what I decided to bring that Mom approved.

1. Travel Journal (see above).

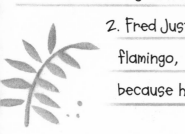

2. Fred Just Fred (my second-favorite flamingo, but don't tell him that because he thinks he's my favorite).

3. *Charlotte's Web* (my favorite book that I have read many times, but I never get tired of reading, but you know that already).

# FLYiNG

This was not my first time on a plane, but it was my first time on a plane for more than two hours. It took over eleven hours to get from Los Angeles to Tokyo. That's like a whole day.

The plane was huge!

"I want to sit by the window," I announced as we walked down the aisle.

"Whatever," Sophie said. "I don't."

I felt sad because Sophie was being Sophie

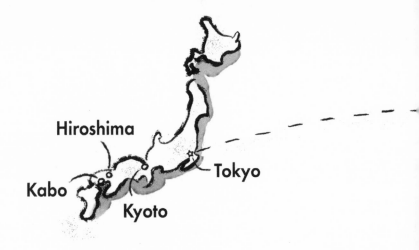

again. She didn't want to do anything I wanted to do. Well! That was fine with me because that meant I didn't have to fight her for the window seat.

"Here we are," Dad said, pointing to a middle row.

"But I wanted to sit by the window," I said.

"The middle row has four seats together," Mom explained. "This way we can all sit as a family."

I tried to sit next to Sophie, but she said, "Not a chance." So I sat on the aisle seat next to Dad, who sat next to Mom, who sat next to

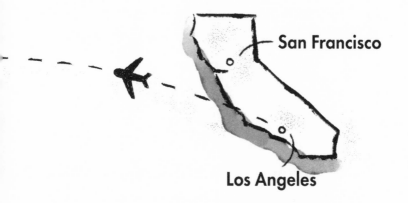

San Francisco

Los Angeles

Sophie, who got the aisle on the other side. She was as far away from me as she could get in our row. That made my heart hurt.

When the plane finally started to rumble down the runway for takeoff, I leaned forward to try to see out the closest window, but the people in that row were blocking my view.

I leaned in front of Dad and Mom. "Hey, Sophie! Look out your window!" At least she had a clear view.

Sophie glared at me and then looked back down at the book she was reading. *Walnuts!* She sure was grumpy.

The plane took off and soon we were flying high up in the sky. I had plenty to keep me busy.

First I wrote in my journal. Then I played with Fred Just Fred. I ate two brownies without nuts that my neighbor Mrs. Reese made for me. Fortunately, Mom did not count snacks as *personal items*. I read two chapters of *Charlotte's Web*. Mom always said keeping busy made the time go by faster.

"How many more hours until we get to Tokyo?" I asked Dad. "Are we almost there?"

Dad laughed and patted my arm. "We just barely took off, sweetie. We have many many hours to go. Why don't you watch a movie?"

We had little screens on the backs of the seats in front of us. My very own TV! But I did not want to watch a movie by myself. "Can I sit next to Sophie?" I asked Dad.

Dad leaned over Mom to talk to Sophie.

"She said okay, but please behave," Dad said.

I always behaved! It was Sophie who got in bad moods for no reason. Mom switched places with me and I settled in next to my sister.

Sophie had the tray down in front of her. It had a pile of books on it. I'd seen her studying Japanese workbooks all summer long. She'd spent most of her summer learning like we were going to school instead of on vacation.

"Why are you studying so hard? We are not going to be tested," I said.

"We will definitely be tested," Sophie said, putting down her pencil and looking at me.

"What? No!" I squeezed Fred Just Fred.

"Well, not like a test in school," she said.

Whew. That was a relief.

"But," Sophie continued, "everyone will be speaking Japanese. And things are different in Japan. They have different customs."

I shook my head. "Obaachan speaks English. Mom and Dad speak Japanese. We don't need to speak Japanese."

Sophie gave me that look that said she was smarter than me. "Maybe. But I like to be prepared."

"It's a vacation. You don't need to prepare!"

"Okay, smarty," Sophie said. She closed her workbook and faced me. "What does gomen nasai mean?"

I rolled my eyes. "Easy," I said. "Excuse me."

"Domo arigato," Sophie said.

"Thank you very much. And doitashi mashite means you're welcome." Sitting with Sophie was not as much fun as I had hoped. This felt like a test, and as much as I liked school, I did not want to study with Sophie. "Let's watch a movie."

"How do you say movie in Japanese?" Sophie asked.

I frowned. "I don't know."

"Movie is eiga in Japanese," Sophie said.

I shrugged.

"Fine," she said. "I'll take a break. But you'll wish you studied with me when we get there."

Sophie loved to study. She loved to show off

how much she knew. She loved to practice and be good at everything.

I didn't need to study because I knew I would love everything about our vacation. I loved adventure!

I curled up with Fred Just Fred. Sophie and I picked the same movie to watch. Even though we had separate screens we watched at the same time. That was nice.

## Jasmine's Journal

Dear Linnie,

The plane ride is too long and very boring. Good thing I have you to talk to. I can't wait until we land in Tokyo and I get to explore. It will be new and exciting. I'm not sure what kind of adventures I will have, but I'm sure they will be special and fun and amazing!

If you were here, we would laugh and talk to each other the entire time. We would want to do the same things at the same time, like when we play with your dog, Trixie, or dress up in costumes at your house or make collages at my house.

I am so bored! There is nothing to do on this plane. Mom is doing

needlepoint. Dad is reading. Sophie is studying.

Oh! Dad just said I can listen to music on his phone. Hooray!

# KONNICHIWA, JAPAN

My bed shook. Was it an earthquake? I tried to get up, but something was holding me down. I rubbed my eyes. Oh. I wasn't in bed at home. I was sitting in an airplane with my seat belt on.

The flight attendant's voice came over the speakers. "Good afternoon and welcome to Narita Airport. It is four thirty p.m." She said a bunch of other things and then switched to Japanese. We were finally here in Tokyo! I tried to wake up. If it was four thirty in the afternoon, why did it feel like the middle of the night? And when had I fallen asleep?

Dad leaned over and nudged me gently. "Jasmine? We're here! We have to get off the plane now."

"I'm awake," I said, all sleepy. It was time for adventure. Normally I would want to hop and jump with energy. But my arms and legs felt super-heavy. "Why am I so tired?"

Dad laughed softly. "Remember, there is a sixteen-hour time difference between Los Angeles and Tokyo."

Oh yes. When we video-chat with Obaachan,

our grandma who lives in Hiroshima, we usually talk at night, when it is morning for her.

"What time

is it at home right now?" I hefted my backpack over my shoulders. I followed Dad into the aisle where people were waiting to get off the plane.

"Subtract sixteen," Sophie said, pushing her way in front of me.

"Hey! No cutting," I said.

"We're all going to get there together," Sophie said. "And it's past midnight at home."

No wonder I was so sleepy. Mom held my hand as I stumbled off the plane. I felt like I was sleepwalking. Maybe I slept a little as we made our way through too many lines: passport control, baggage claim, and customs.

We got on a train to take us into Tokyo and to our hotel. The train was super-clean and quiet with comfortable seats. We were finally in Japan, but the train was not that special. I fell asleep against Dad's shoulder.

When we made it into Tokyo and stepped off the train, I suddenly felt awake. There were so many people in the train station. I

出口↑ | EXIT

←

gripped Mom's arm
with one hand as I
rolled my suitcase with my
other. I whipped my head side to
side, taking everything in. The announcements were in Japanese, but the
signs above us were in both Japanese and

English. There
were many post-
ers and bright screens
with video clips on the
columns. I saw restaurants, a
bakery, and shops. It was not that
different from a mall back home. Except

the stores here looked very different and interesting. I wanted to explore!

"Mom," I said. "Can we look in a store?"

"Not now, sweetie. We are going to check in to our hotel."

I glanced at Mom. She looked sleepy, too. When would my adventure start?

We walked and walked and walked, and finally, we made it outside. The sun was starting to go down. I could hardly see the sky because it was filled with tall buildings. There were so many cars! Even though Los Angeles is a city with a lot of people and cars, we lived on a quiet street with not a lot of traffic.

"What are we going to do after the hotel?" I asked.

"Tonight we are going to eat dinner and get settled in," Dad said, stopping at the crosswalk. "We will get a fresh start tomorrow."

*Walnuts!* I wanted to explore now!

It turned out that our hotel was across the street from the train station. Good thing. I was tired of dragging my suitcase.

The hotel was shiny and smelled good, but it looked a lot like other hotels we've stayed at. We took the elevator up to our room. The elevator looked just like the ones we had back home, too.

When we got to our room, the windows took up one whole wall. *Wowee zowee!* The view was amazing! There were many buildings all lit up like stars in the sky.

"Sophie!" I said. "Come look out the window. It is so pretty outside."

If looks could kill, I'd be dead from Sophie's glare. Instead of standing with me at the window, she curled up on the bed we were going to share.

"If you fall asleep now," Dad said to her, "it will be even harder to get adjusted to the time in Japan. It's better to stay awake. It's dinner-time. Let's go eat."

"Eat? It feels like the middle of the night," Sophie said.

I checked the clock on the nightstand. "It's seven o'clock. Way past dinner. I'm hungry."

Maybe now we would have an adventure!

# RAMEN STREET

I couldn't wait for dinner! I had never had a meal in Japan before. I didn't know what to expect, but I knew it would be fabulous.

Dad led us back into the train station. *Walnuts!* I wanted to see something new. Then we got in a long line.

"Is this for the train?" I peered around, trying to see what was at the front of the line.

"Nope," Dad said. "This is Ramen Street."

*Wowee zowee!* A whole street made of ramen? My adventure was finally starting! "Will our feet get wet walking in soup?"

Dad laughed and ruffled my hair. "Ramen Street is the name of this section in the train station. There are eight ramen shops here serving different types of ramen."

"Oh." I was disappointed we weren't going to see a street made of ramen. Also I had eaten ramen many times before. Good thing I loved ramen.

Sophie pushed her way next to me. She used her teacher voice to say, "Did you know that different regions of Japan specialize in different ramen? Not all ramen is the same."

Sophie was definitely more awake now. I guessed being able to show off how much she knew made her not so sleepy anymore.

By the time we got to the front of the line, my stomach was making rumbling sounds. I was glad we would eat soon. But instead of getting seated at a table, we stood in front of a vending machine.

"Does our food come out of here?" I asked, squinting at the brightly lit buttons. Each button had a picture of ramen on it.

"We choose what we want from this machine and get tickets. We give the tickets to our server when we sit down," Mom explained.

Well, that was different. "I want to push the buttons," I said.

"No. I'm older. I should get to push the buttons," Sophie said.

That didn't make sense. Why would being older mean you get to push buttons? I peered closer at the machine.

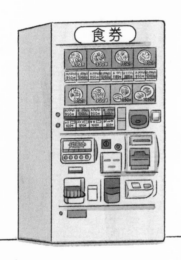

"It's a thousand dollars for ramen?" I asked.

"No, silly," Sophie said. "In Japan the money is called yen. Don't you know anything?"

I made a face at her.

"Girls, please use good manners and be kind," Dad said. "A thousand yen equals about ten dollars, Jasmine."

"I'll order for us." Mom pushed a bunch of buttons, and then put money into the slot.

"There's an open table," I said, pointing.

"Don't point," Sophie said. "It's very rude in Japan."

That seemed like a made-up rule. I glanced at Mom. She was the queen of rules. She would know for sure.

Mom nodded. "It's rude anywhere, but especially in Japan."

Hmm. I guessed Sophie did know what she was talking about. I'd try to remember not to point.

By the time we sat down, I was super-hungry. The server took our tickets and said some stuff in Japanese to Mom and Dad. I couldn't wait for my food.

The server returned and put a big bowl of ramen in front of each of us.

I peeked into my bowl. It didn't look like the ramen I had at home. The soup was light-colored and there was a boiled egg and meat that looked yummy. But there was also some other stuff I didn't recognize.

"Those are bamboo shoots," Sophie said. "And nori."

I liked nori. The first time I shared nori with Linnie, I told her it was seaweed and she scrunched her nose. But then she tried it and she loved it.

This ramen was not what I was expecting.

I watched Sophie eat the bamboo shoot. She was usually not very adventurous. I did not want her to be more adventurous than me. I picked up the bamboo shoot with my hashi and nibbled. It was a little chewy, but I liked it. I started eating my noodles quickly.

Sophie didn't need to tell me that it was polite to slurp noodles in Japan. I knew that already.

After we ate our delicious dinner, we walked through the train station.

"Can we look in the stores?" I asked.

"Let's head back to our room," Mom said. "I'm about to fall asleep on my feet."

I wished we could start our vacation now, but I guessed tomorrow would have to do.

Back in our room with my full belly, I was ready to sleep. Mom made us brush our teeth and wash our faces before letting us change into our pajamas. I picked up Fred Just Fred and hugged him as I crawled into the bed I was sharing with Sophie. It was right next to the window where I could see the night sky.

I remembered how Dad said we should be kind.

"You can sleep next to the window, Sophie."

"Leave me alone," Sophie said. She was tired and grouchy.

"I am trying to be kind, like Dad said. You should learn to be kind!" Maybe I was a little tired and grouchy, too.

"Move over," Sophie said.

Even though she shoved me, she let me have the side of the bed next to the window.

"Oyasuminasai," I said, just to show her that I knew how to say good night in Japanese even though I didn't spend all summer studying.

## Jasmine's Journal

Dear Linnie,

I am trying to write fast. Sophie is complaining about the light being on. We are sharing a bed and she is not happy about it. She just put up a row of pillows between us. She told me it's because I kick in my sleep. I do not kick in my sleep! I'm sure you would have said something by now since we sleep next to each other in our sleeping bags during sleepovers.

Sophie→ →jasmine

I want to tell you about Tokyo, but there really isn't much to say yet. Tomorrow will be our big adventure day! I want to make a list of all the things I want to do, but Sophie just told me I have two seconds before she turns off the light.

# SUBWAY

JAPAN AIRLINES ✈
TOGUCHI/ JASMINE
FLIGHT JL 61
FROM LOS ANGELES-LAX USA
TO TOKYO-NRT JAPAN

Jépan
TOGUCHI/JASMINE
FROM LAX
TO NRT
FLIGHT DATE
JL 61 08/22
SEAT GATE
17G 132

"Girls, you need to wake up."

Mom's voice sounded very far away. My eyes wouldn't open. I snuggled deeper under the covers.

Suddenly something sharp jabbed my side.

"Ow!" I squeaked. My eyes flew open and I sat up. I rubbed my ribs. The sharp thing that had poked me was Sophie's elbow. The pillows she put up for protection against my feet were on the floor. I was the one who needed protection. I thought about jabbing her back, but then I remembered why we were sharing a bed.

"Sophie, Sophie! Wake up! We're in Japan! Ohayo gozai masu!" I shouted good morning.

Mom laughed and hugged me. "It's actually almost noon. We let you both sleep in, but now we need to get moving. I brought up some pastries from the breakfast buffet."

I hurried over to the table, excited to see what was for breakfast. Oh. It was a chocolate doughnut that looked like any other doughnut from home. At least it was yummy.

Mom dragged Sophie to the bathroom, telling her a shower would help her wake up. It didn't seem to work. She was still pretty sleepy after her shower.

"Hey, Sophie, you should pay attention to

our vacation," I said while she bit into her doughnut.

"You are getting crumbs all over the place," I said. That was not like Sophie. Usually she was the neat one telling me to not be messy.

Sophie did not say anything back to me, which was also not like her. But her eyes were still half closed like she was eating in her sleep.

Dad walked into the room. He had been at a meeting with a professor at a college in Tokyo. Dad teaches history at a college in Los Angeles. I guessed teachers liked talking to each other.

"Ready for an adventure?" Dad asked in a loud, cheerful voice.

"Yes!" I shouted. "What are we doing today?"

We were spending two whole days in Tokyo before we took a train to Hiroshima to visit our grandma. Mom and Dad were letting us each pick one thing that we wanted to do. I hoped we were doing my thing today.

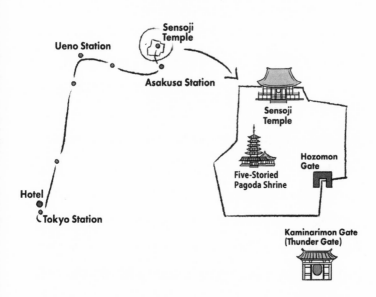

"We are taking the subway to Asakusa, a district in Tokyo where there is a big temple," Dad said.

Sophie suddenly looked very awake. She jumped out of her chair and cheered. Then she turned to me and said, "Ha-ha! We're doing *my* thing first!"

"No fair!" I said.

"Don't worry, Jasmine," Mom said. "We will go to Tokyo Tower tomorrow."

I made a face at Sophie, but she was too busy putting on her shoes to see me.

We ended up back at Tokyo Station. This time we were taking the subway. I followed Dad to the platform. The subway shushed into the station. Everyone stood in silent lines and waited until people got off before getting on. Except for the announcements, it was pretty quiet.

We found two seats. Mom and Sophie sat because I wanted to stand with Dad. I was too short to hold on to the hanging-strap thing, but I could hold on to the pole. As the subway moved, I leaned to keep my balance. It was fun!

"How long will it take to get there?" I asked. "Sophie, aren't you excited? Why do you want to see this temple? Is there something special

about it you like? I'm so glad we are all together having a big adventure!"

Sophie scrunched her nose at me.

"What?" I was full of energy. I wanted to
hop up and down, but the subway car was
pretty crowded. I didn't want to bump into
anyone.

"Jasmine," Sophie said in a whisper. "In
Japan, you don't speak on the subway. Can't
you see you're the only one talking?"

I glanced around. Sophie was right. It was as quiet as a library. People were reading books or looking at their phones. Kids like me were sitting silently. My face got hot. How was I supposed to know this rule? I looked at Mom. She gave me a small smile and nodded.

I waited for Sophie to scold me. She loved doing that. She definitely knew more than I did about Japan. But Sophie was reading a book, looking like all the other people on the subway. Like she belonged.

# SNACK TiME

The subway ride took forever. Mom and Dad were on their phones. Sophie read her book. I had nothing to do because nobody had told me to bring my book. I could not talk. That was very hard! In our car, I counted people to pass the time. Ichi, ni, two businessmen in suits. Ichi, ni, san, shi, four students in school uniforms. I looked at the posters and signs in the subway car but they were all in Japanese.

Finally finally finally, we got to our stop. I

held Dad's hand as we got off. Once we made it outside to the street, I asked, "Am I allowed to talk now?"

"You're allowed to talk, Jasmine," Mom said, "but try to do it quietly and only if necessary on the subway."

It was always necessary when I had something to say, but I would try to talk less on the subway.

As we walked, my shirt got damp from sweat. It was super-hot and sticky. It was so hot and sticky that I didn't want to hold Dad's hand anymore. I let go and skipped ahead.

"Matte!" Dad called.

I didn't know what that meant so I kept skipping. Even though it was hot the air felt good as my ponytail swished and bounced.

"Jasmine!" Sophie caught up to me. "Dad said to wait."

"How was I supposed to know?" I asked.

"If you had studied before we came, you

would know stuff. Like not talking on the subway and not pointing and what matte means."

It was hard to remember the rules in Japan. They were not the same as back home. Sophie and I slowed down to let Mom and Dad catch up with us, and we all walked together to the temple. It looked like everyone around us was going there, too.

"Why did you choose this place for your thing to do in Tokyo?" I asked Sophie.

"Well," she said, "I really wanted to see Mount Fuji because it's famous, but Mom and Dad said we don't have time to do that this trip. I did a lot of research and Sensoji Temple is one of the most popular and well-known places in Tokyo. And it is the oldest temple in Tokyo. The pictures of it were awesome. And I have never been to a Buddhist temple before."

I had never been to a temple before either, but knowing Sophie, it was something to be studied. Something to learn. That sounded boring. I was just about to tell her so when suddenly Sophie stopped walking. In front of us was a little building with tall columns and a fancy roof. Hanging right in the center was a ginormous red lantern with Japanese kanji in black written on it.

"This is the Kaminarimon," Mom said.

"That means Thunder Gate," Sophie said.

Whoa. It was the fanciest and biggest gate I'd ever seen, that was for sure. I wished our gate to the backyard at home looked like this. That would be awesome!

We walked through the gate onto a long road crammed full of people. It was like the whole city was here today. Lots of shops selling souvenirs and food lined either side of the road.

"What's going on there?" I asked, pointing at a crowd. Then I remembered that pointing was rude, so I lowered my hand.

I followed my nose to something delicious. Sophie, Mom, and Dad followed me. I stopped at the group of people looking in a window. Inside was a man standing at a grill. He spooned batter in perfect circles, like cookies, onto the grill. Then he took a little spatula and flipped them over to cook. Oh! They were little pancakes, golden brown.

A few people stepped in front of me and I

couldn't see very well anymore. I peeked between two women and watched the man take
two pancakes and smear chocolate between
them! YUM!

"Can we get a snack?" I asked Mom.

She smiled. "Yes! I love dorayaki. Dad already got in line to order some for us."

It smelled so sweet and delicious. I couldn't wait to bite
into fluffy, chocolate-filled
pancakes!

Dad joined us and handed

me a warm pancake sandwich in a white paper wrapper. I started to walk back down the shopping street, but Mom stopped me.

"It's not polite to eat while walking," Mom explained. Another new rule I didn't know about. It was confusing not knowing things.

Mom nodded her head to where a few people were huddled next to the side of the shop, eating their dorayaki. We stood with them, and I bit into my chocolate pancake. I chewed. Wait. This wasn't chocolate!

"It's anpan!" I exclaimed. It was a sweet paste made from azuki. The red beans are my favorite mochi filling.

"What did you think it was?" Sophie asked with her mouth full.

I did not point out that she was being rude. Maybe in Japan it was okay to talk with your mouth full? There were a lot of things I didn't know—the manners, the language, the city, and now, the food.

Not knowing so many things made my stomach wobbly, like I was walking on a tightrope. I thought I knew a lot about Japan, but maybe I didn't.

Sophie had studied all summer to know things, but at least now I knew about dorayaki. Even though I had never had it before, it tasted familiar. Dad made pancakes at home every Sunday. Azuki was my favorite mochi filling. The flavors of pancakes and azuki together were delicious. I gobbled up my treat and felt a little better.

# SENSOJI TEMPLE

Once we finished our yummy dorayaki, we walked past the shops to the end of the street. There was another gate but it was even bigger than the first one we had passed under.

"Wowee zowee," I said, craning my neck to look up at it. This one was two stories tall! It also had a giant red lantern hanging from the entryway.

"This is the Hozomon," Mom said. "This gate leads into the main grounds of the temple."

As we passed under it, I looked up.

"Dragons!" I shouted.

"Ooh," Sophie said. "That's so awesome."

Dad looked at his phone. "This area used to be prone to fires, so the dragons were carved into the bottom of the lantern to protect the temple."

"What do you mean?" I asked. "That doesn't make sense. Don't they breathe fire?"

"You're thinking of European dragons," Mom said. "Asian dragons are considered to be water deities. So they would protect against fire."

"Wowee zowee!"

We walked over to a big statue of a man with a dragon perched on his shoulders. He held a closed umbrella like a cane. I guess in case the dragon started spitting water. More dragons surrounded his feet and water poured out from their mouths into a fountain.

Dad showed me what to do. I held the metal scoop under one of the dragons until my scoop was filled with water. Then I poured the water over each hand to clean them. The cool water felt good.

Our next stop was a big metal bowl with smoke coming from it.

"This is a jokoro, or an incense burner," Mom explained. "It is thought that the smoke from the burning incense sticks cleanses the body."

We used our hands to waft smoke toward us. Who knew getting clean could be so fun?

We climbed the steps to the temple, where we saw flowers and gold statues. Once we were done exploring, we stopped at a stand selling things near the temple. Sophie's eyes got bright. She loved shopping.

"What are these?" Sophie asked Mom.

I guessed she didn't know everything after all. That made me feel a little better.

"Oh! These are omamori," Mom said. "They are good-luck charms."

"Cool!" There were many charms, each

hanging from a cord. They were flat silk pouches in different colors with Japanese writing on them. I would get one and hang it on my backpack!

"Each one is a charm for something specific," Dad explained. "This one is for happiness, and this one is for good health. There are ones for love, money, and even for homework or tests."

Mom picked up two.

"What are those for?" I asked.

"Safe driving. I will hang one in each of our cars."

"Are you getting one?" I asked Sophie.

She nodded as she looked over her choices. "I'm going to get the one for success. Maybe it will help me in school."

I didn't think she needed it. Sophie was very smart and always did her homework and got great grades. But she was starting middle school in the fall, so maybe she was nervous.

"Can I get one for good luck?" I asked. That seemed like a wowee-zowee idea.

"Of course," Dad said.

I also got charms for each of my friends at home: Linnie, Daisy, Tommy, Maggie, and Mrs. Reese. Everyone could use a bit of luck.

I tucked my omamori in my backpack next to Fred Just Fred.

I was excited to see Obaachan and explore a lot of new places. But most of all I wanted to be friends with Sophie. I hoped my omamori would give me good luck.

## Jasmine's Journal

Dear Linnie,

I wish you could really be here, even though it's fun to talk to you in this journal. Sophie is either bossy (telling me everything she knows about things I don't know) or grouchy (even crabbier than usual). It would be much more fun if Sophie and I were friends.

Tomorrow we are going to Tokyo Tower. It is super-tall and I am excited to see all of Tokyo from high up in the sky, like maybe if I were a flying flamingo.

Finally my adventure will start!

# BREAKFAST
# SURPRISE

The sunlight streaming into the hotel-room windows woke me up. I threw the covers off

and leaped out of bed. I jumped up and down and sang, "Ohayo gozai masu!"

I was in Tokyo and today was *my* day!

Mom and Dad were already up and

dressed. Dad was typing something on his laptop. Mom was reading her book.

"Wake up, Sophie," I said. "We're going to Tokyo Tower!"

Sophie groaned and pulled the covers over her head.

I bounced next to her, pushing away the wall of pillows that protected me from her sharp elbows.

"Come on!" I said. I pulled the covers off her.

"Jasmine! Stop! Leave me alone!" Sophie glared at me. Her hair was in a big tangle. She was scary-looking.

"You are going to miss out on all the fun if you're crabby all the time," I said, hugging Fred Just Fred.

Sophie growled, and I quickly scrambled off the bed to get dressed. When Mom finally got Sophie up and moving, we went downstairs to eat at the hotel's breakfast buffet.

Mom and Dad got our food for us since it

might have been hard for us to balance our trays. My tray was filled with a million little dishes. A feast! My tummy rumbled. I picked up my hashi, trying to decide where to start. Except I didn't know what most of the things on my tray were. I squinted at the dishes, leaning my head right and left, hoping that would make the food look familiar.

I did not see doughnuts or cereal or bacon or toast. I did not even see those yummy pancakes we had yesterday.

"Why are you just sitting there?" Sophie asked. She used her chopsticks to pick up a tamago.

I knew what that was! I loved Japanese omelet—it was rolled and sliced, a little sweet and a little salty. I popped one in my mouth. Mmm.

"Oishii desu," Sophie said.

"That means it tastes good," I said. "See? I can understand Japanese."

Now that I had a better look at my

breakfast, I recognized most of the food after all. There was a little dish full of edamame. I loved popping the soybeans from the pod into my mouth. One time Sophie and I popped the beans at each other in an edamame war. Mom did not approve.

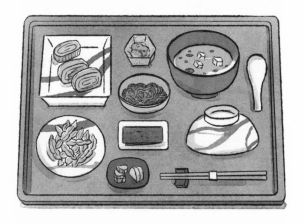

There was miso soup in a black bowl on my tray. I drank it Japanese style, without a spoon. I knew that in Japan it was polite to lift your bowl to your mouth to drink soup. Then I used my hashi to pick out the pieces of tofu and wakame from the bowl.

Japanese breakfasts were different from

the kinds of breakfasts I ate at home. But I loved Japanese food! Sophie told me all about the different food. I already knew everything she said, but I pretended not to. It seemed like she was in a better mood. This made me happy!

When we were finished eating breakfast, it was time to leave for Tokyo Tower.

"Are you excited?" I asked Sophie as we walked to the subway.

"Leave me alone, Jasmine." Sophie stalked ahead and caught up to Dad.

I did not understand how she went from happy one moment (maybe because she liked showing off how much she knew?) to grouchy the next. I was too excited about my adventure to think more about it.

This time I was ready for the subway. I remembered not to talk. At least not much and not loudly. I read a new manga in English that I bought at a bookstore last night.

Before I knew it, we were there! Tokyo Tower!

"Wowee zowee!" I said when we got to the base of the red-and-white tower. I leaned back and looked up up up at the tall tall tower. It was beautiful. I couldn't wait to go to the top.

Fortunately the signs were in both English

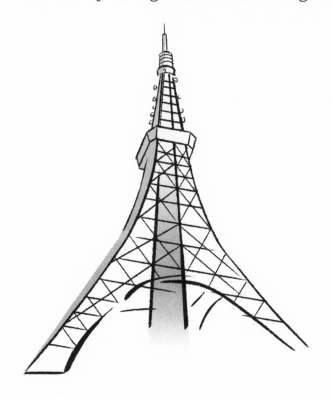

and Japanese. "The entrance and tickets are over there," I said without pointing.

I pulled on Mom's hand and led the way. Inside was cool and air-conditioned. It felt wonderful. We waited in line, but this time I didn't mind because I was so excited that we would soon be at the top and looking at a wonderful view of Tokyo. I turned to smile at my sister, but she was not smiling.

"This will be fun," I said.

She glared at me. Then she turned her head away. I was not going to let Sophie's bad attitude ruin the best day ever!

# HAPPY DAY
# (BUT NOT FOR SOPHiE)

Once we got our tickets, we followed the path to another line of people. So many lines to wait in. But at least this one led to the elevator.

This was it! We were going to the top of Tokyo Tower. I was so excited I couldn't help myself. I hopped on my left foot twice and my right foot three times while holding on to Dad's hand.

"Watch it!" Sophie said, nudging me. "You almost stepped on my foot!"

*Walnuts!* Sophie was still crabby with me. Maybe it was because she was sleepy. I looked at the brochure for the tower. We were going to the Main Deck, which was 150 meters high.

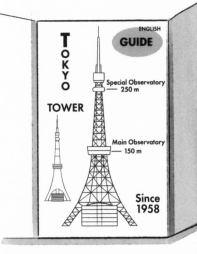

"Dad? What's 150 meters?"

"Hmm." Dad tapped on his phone. "About 492 feet."

I scrunched my nose.

"Hang on," Mom said, looking on her phone. "Okay. An adult greater flamingo is about 5 feet tall. So that means 150 meters is like stacking 98 flamingos on top of each other."

"Wowee zowee! That's tall!" I looked at the brochure again. "The very top deck is 250 meters."

"Stop," Sophie said in a small voice. "Stop talking about how high up we are going to be."

When I looked at Sophie, her face was scrunched like she didn't feel well. Maybe that was why she was crabby. Maybe she didn't like the rocking of the subway ride or it was too hot for her. I was going to say something back to Sophie. Her being so mean was ruining my happy adventure. But then Mom squeezed my hand. I think she was telling me I was doing a good job by not teasing Sophie.

We got into the elevator. I pressed my face against the glass. I watched the ground get

farther and farther away. I glanced at Sophie. She had her back to the glass and was holding Dad's hand super-tight.

When the elevator doors opened, we followed the group of people out and I ran to the wall of windows to see Tokyo spread out below us. The buildings that were super-tall when we were walking on the street now looked short. I could see the tops of those buildings. I made my way around the windows so I could see all the views of Tokyo. I saw trees that looked like they were from a dollhouse. I watched the cars, which looked like toys as they drove on the streets below us.

Sophie followed along, but not close to the windows. She kept her eyes down as she held Dad's hand. She was missing out.

"Sophie, come see!"

She gave me a super-glare.

"You won't fall out," I said.

Sophie stalked to a chair, her ponytail

bouncing, and sat down hard with her arms crossed.

I felt anger bubble up in me. I stood in front of her. "Just because it's my turn to do my thing, you do not have to be so mean! I was nice yesterday even though we did your thing first."

"Do not even talk to me," Sophie said.

"Jasmine," Mom said, taking my hand.

"Come this way, I want to show you something you will love."

What could be better than looking out the windows?

Mom pointed to the floor.

*Wowee zowee!* It was a window in the floor!

"Can we stand on it?" I asked.

"We can." Mom stepped on the glass and I followed her. I would not be hopping and jumping here, even though I was full of energy and happiness.

I looked down and my heart pounded hard in my chest like a taiko drum. *Boom! Boom! Boom!* I was floating in the air. I took Fred Just Fred out of my backpack and held him over the window in the floor so he could feel like he was flying.

At home, our neighbor Mrs. Reese lets me climb her apricot tree whenever I want. I loved being high up. It made me feel tall and powerful. I was the only one who used Mrs. Reese's tree. Sophie wouldn't climb it, which is fine by me since it's *my* private thinking spot. Linnie didn't like climbing it either, because she is afraid of being high up.

Oh.

I thought back to all the times on our vacation that Sophie had been extra-mean to me. When I told her to look out the airplane window. When I offered to let her have the side of the bed next to the hotel window. And here, as we were high up in Tokyo Tower. She wasn't being mean because she didn't like me. She was being mean because she was afraid.

"Sophie would not like this," I said to Mom.

"No, she would not," she said softly.

I didn't understand. It was awesome to be high in the sky and look at everything down below us. Sophie was silly. And not very brave, like I was.

Mom and I started walking back to where Dad and Sophie were sitting. I saw a vending machine. Japan had a lot of vending machines.

"Wait, Mom," I said. "What is in this machine?" It did not look like drinks or snacks. It did not look like tickets for ramen.

I peered in the windows of the machine. Inside were shiny medals with an image of Tokyo Tower!

"Can we get one?" I asked.

"Sure," Mom said. "It's a nice souvenir."

Mom handed money to me. I loved the money in Japan. The bills were bright and colorful. The coins were even better. Some of them had a hole in the center.

I knew which color medal I was going to

get. I put in the
money and picked
the purple one.
The medal made
a happy clinking
sound as it fell to
the bottom of the
machine. It felt cool
in my hands. I held it

up and smiled. It was like I had won a bravery
medal for being in Tokyo Tower.

All of a sudden I got an idea.

# THE BIG REWARD

I pressed my face against the vending machine window, looking carefully at each medal.

"Mom?" I asked. "Can I get one for Sophie, too?"

"That's very nice of you, Jasmine." Mom smiled and handed me more money.

I picked the very special hologram one for my sister. And now to put my plan into action! I walked over to Sophie.

"Hey," I said, sitting next to Sophie.

Dad got up to look around since he hadn't yet gotten a chance to explore the tower. Mom went to the café to get something to drink.

Sophie kept her head down, staring at her sandals.

"I got you something," I said.

Sophie peeked up at me through her hair. I handed her the medal.

She tilted it back and forth to see the image. Even though it had a picture of Tokyo Tower on it, she seemed to like it.

"It's a bravery medal," I said.

She squinted at me, like she thought I was making fun of her.

"It will make you feel brave. When we go to

the next level, maybe you will be able to look out the windows."

Sophie rubbed the medal with her thumbs.

I thought about telling her that she shouldn't be afraid of heights. That we would not fall out of the tower. I thought about my best friend, Linnie, and how sometimes she was afraid of the dark or climbing, just like Sophie. I never made Linnie do things she was afraid to do. I shouldn't make Sophie either. She couldn't help being afraid.

"You know what?" I said to Sophie. "You don't have to go up to the next level. I'll bet Mom would stay with you or maybe you can go downstairs and wait for us."

Sophie clutched her medal. She took a deep breath. "I read in the brochure that sometimes you can see Mount Fuji from Tokyo Tower."

"Oh!" I exclaimed. "That's right. You said you wanted to see Mount Fuji!"

When Mom and Dad came to get us, I glanced at Sophie. She peered over at me and nodded once. She held Dad's hand and with her other hand she held the medal I gave her. After another long elevator ride we made it to the very top deck.

"I can't look." Sophie covered her eyes and stopped in the middle of the floor. People had to walk around her, but they didn't seem to mind. Mom stood with Sophie and nodded for me and Dad to go on. I pressed my face to the windows.

We were even higher up! Way *way* up! Everything below looked even smaller. Teeny-tiny cars moved like ants on a trail.

Something touched my arm. It was Sophie. Her eyes were still scrunched shut, but she was holding my arm with one hand and her medal with the other.

"Take a peek, Sophie," I said. "You can do it."

"I can't," she whispered. "Can you see Mount Fuji?"

I looked out across Tokyo, above the tops of buildings. "No."

"I think it's on the opposite side," Dad said.

"Sophie, it's rare to have such a clear day. Most days it is too hazy to see that far. We should be able to see Mount Fuji."

"It's your lucky day, Sophie," I exclaimed.

Sophie held on to my arm and I guided her to the other side of the platform.

"We're here."

Sophie took a deep shaky breath and opened her eyes, being careful not to look down. She frowned. "I don't see anything."

Dad nodded. "Look farther out, Sophie. It's a little hard to see, but that brown smudge way in the distance is Mount Fuji."

Sophie seemed to forget about how high up she was as she leaned against the window, staring out at the sky. Then she grinned. "I see it!"

I looked where she was looking. Dad was right. Far off in the distance was a brown smudge, but it was definitely there. "What a pretty mountain," I said.

Sophie looked at me and huffed. "It's not a mountain," she said, using her teacher voice.

"It's a volcano. And the Japanese people call it Fuji-san as a sign of respect."

"Wowee zowee," I said. "That's awesome, Sophie!"

I smiled at her and she smiled back.

Sophie was not brave like me. She was afraid of the dark. She didn't like scary movies or being high up.

Now I understood why she wanted to study the Japanese language and everything about Japan. Knowing things made her feel less afraid.

It was true that I hadn't spent my summer studying. And I wished I knew as much as Sophie did. But I got to play and have fun all summer.

Now Sophie could tell me everything I needed to know. Sometimes it was a good thing to have an older sister who knew more than I did.

I thought about how things were a lot different here than I expected. There were new rules and special ways of doing things, but I loved adventure.

Maybe Sophie and I could both try to learn new things together.

My sister held my hand as we walked back to the elevator. "I'm glad we came," Sophie said. "Thank you for the bravery medal, Jasmine."

My heart floated higher than Tokyo Tower.

That's when I knew for sure Sophie and I would have a great time exploring Japan together! This was going to be the best vacation ever!

Jasmine's Journal

Dear Linnie,

Tokyo has been fun and interesting, but there were some things I was not expecting.

The food is not the same here. Like ramen in Japan has different toppings and there were treats that looked like pancakes but were kind of like mochi. I still tried them. Guess what? They were delicious!

Rules and manners are different in Japan. Like no talking on subways. But I listened to Sophie, and I learned. And now I know not to point, and not to eat while walking.

And when Sophie was being super-mean to me, I had to figure out why. After I figured out that she was afraid of being high up, I

gave her a present that made her feel better and braver.

I thought my adventure started when we finally went to the top of Tokyo Tower, but I was wrong. I've been a brave explorer all along!

And I will have more adventures. Tomorrow we are getting on a super-fast train—to finally visit Obaachan in Hiroshima. I can't wait!

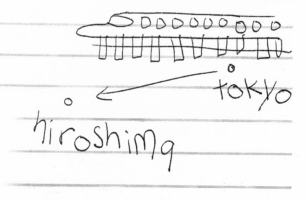

# AUTHOR'S NOTE

Jasmine and her family often eat meals with chopsticks, called hashi (HAH-shee) in Japanese.

It is believed that the Chinese people first used chopsticks over 5,000 years ago and that they were introduced to Japan around 500 CE. Japanese chopsticks are typically pointed and are made of lacquered wood—painted with a shiny coating. The Japanese people were the first to lacquer chopsticks. Disposable chopsticks were invented in Japan in the late 1800s.

There are rules (of course) for good manners when it comes to eating with chopsticks. Here are some that Jasmine follows:

• Use your chopsticks for eating. They are not toys. Do not use them as drumsticks to hit the table or plates and glasses.

• If you want to pass food to a friend or family member, place the food item on the other person's plate. Do not pass food directly from chopsticks to chopsticks. This is similar to a funeral ritual (passing cremated bones), so it is considered rude to do that with food.

• When you are not using your chopsticks, place them parallel to each other on a chopstick holder or plate. Do not stick them straight up in your food. That would look like incense in a burner, which is also associated with funerals.

• Do not point with your chopsticks.

# HOW TO EAT WITH
# CHOPSTICKS

Use whichever hand is more comfortable for you.

1. Rest one chopstick across the crook of your thumb and on your third finger.

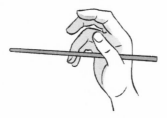

2. Use your middle finger to hold it steady.

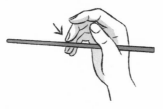

3. Grasp the other chopstick between your middle finger and your pointer finger. This is the upper stick. Use your thumb to hold it steady.

**4.** Move the upper stick so that the tips of the chopsticks come together to pick up a piece of food. The lower stick should not move.

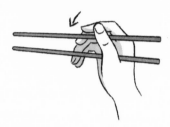

With practice you can use chopsticks to eat your meals.

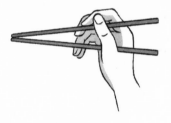

Enjoy!

# DORAYAKI RECIPE

## ALWAYS BE SURE TO HAVE A GROWN-UP HELP YOU!

## INGREDIENTS

- 2 large eggs
- ⅓ cup granulated sugar
- 1 tablespoon honey
- ¾ cup all-purpose flour
- ½ teaspoon baking powder
- ½ tablespoon water
- ½ teaspoon canola oil
- 1 can (15 oz) azuki (sweet red bean) paste

**Note: Azuki can be purchased in Asian grocery stores or online.**

## UTENSILS

One large bowl, measuring cups and measuring spoons, whisk, large sieve for sifting flour, nonstick frying pan, paper towels, large spoon or small ladle or small cup, cooking spatula, timer, large plate, regular spoon, plastic wrap.

## INSTRUCTIONS

1. Whisk the eggs, sugar, and honey together in the large bowl until very well mixed.

2. Sift the flour and baking powder into the bowl that has the eggs, sugar, and honey in it. Mix until the flour and baking powder are combined with the liquid.

3. Cover the bowl with plastic wrap. Place in the refrigerator for about 15 minutes, which will help smooth out the batter.

4. Remove the bowl from the refrigerator. Mix in the water. Set aside.

5. With an adult's help, place the nonstick frying pan on the stove and set to low heat. Allow the pan to warm up (approximately 5 minutes). Pour the canola oil into the pan and spread it to coat the bottom of the pan evenly. Use a piece of paper towel to wipe up the excess oil so the pancakes won't cook unevenly or burn.

6. Measure 3 tablespoons of batter into a large spoon, ladle, or small cup, and pour the batter into the warm frying pan to create a 3-inch circle. When bubbles start to form on top of the pancake (after approximately 1 minute and 30 seconds), flip it over with the

spatula. Let cook for about 30 more seconds and then remove from the pan and place on the plate.

7. Continue cooking the pancakes one at a time until all the batter is gone.

8. Spread the azuki paste between two pancakes, forming a "sandwich."

9. Eat immediately or store individually in plastic wrap. Keep in a cool, dry place. Eat within two days.

Turn the page for a sneak peek of . . .

JASMINE TOGUCHI

PEACE-MAKER

DEBBI MICHIKO FLORENCE    PICTURES BY ELIZABET VUKOVIĆ

BE SURE TO LOOK FOR

JASMINE TOGUCHI
PEACE-MAKER
COMING SOON!

# TO OBAACHAN'S HOUSE WE GO!

The Tokyo train station was big. Very big! I followed Mom and Dad while dragging my suitcase behind me.

I, Jasmine Toguchi, was on the adventure of my life. I flew on a plane with my family all the way from our home in Los Angeles to Japan for a vacation. We spent two days in Tokyo doing fun things and eating yummy food. The best part so far was that my sister, Sophie, was mostly being nice to me. Normally Sophie, who is two years older than me, is bossy and doesn't like to hang out together. But now it seemed she liked spending time with me. It was as if Japan was magical and made wonderful things happen!

Today we were leaving Tokyo to go to Hiroshima to visit Obaachan. Usually we only see our grandma in January when she comes to our house for New Year's and stays for a whole month. This will be the first time we are visiting *her*! We walked and walked (there is a lot of walking to do in Japan) until at last we made it to our gate on the train platform.

"Did you know the Shinkansen is super-fast?" Sophie said in her teacher voice. It used to bother me. But now that Sophie was nicer to me, I liked learning from her. "Some people call it the bullet train."

"How fast does it go?" I asked.

"Fast," Sophie said.

Just as I was about to say that wasn't a good answer, our train pulled in. I couldn't wait to

board. I wanted to go super-fast! I followed Mom and Dad and Sophie onto the train, and we found our seats. Dad moved the backs of the seats so that we could all face one another. Sophie let me have the window seat. This made me happy. Not only was I having a great adventure like I wanted, but Sophie and I were finally friends. Everything was perfect!

I hugged Fred Just Fred and stared out the window. Fred Just Fred is my second-favorite stuffed flamingo. My first favorite is Felicia, but Mom wouldn't let me bring her because she is just as tall as I am. I could see now that it would have been hard to carry her around. Like I said, we do a lot of walking in Japan.

The train pulled out of the station. We passed tall silver buildings and streets full of cars and more buildings. It seemed like we would never leave Tokyo. I waited and watched and waited and watched. After a long while there were fewer buildings and more open spaces.

"We're going fast!" I said as the train picked

up speed. "But it doesn't feel like it." The train was smooth and quiet.

"What are we going to do at Obaachan's?" I asked once the train was racing along outside of Tokyo. Fields and little houses flew by in a blur.

Mom looked up from her book and smiled. "We have some fun plans," she said. "But I think you will both enjoy spending time with Akari."

"Who is that?" Sophie asked.

"She is my cousin's daughter," Mom said. "She's a year older than Sophie and speaks English. Her father speaks both Japanese and English, so Akari has grown up speaking both languages."

"Awesome!" Sophie said.

"What is she like?" I asked. I hoped she enjoyed adventures, too.

"I haven't seen her since she was a baby," Mom said. "You'll have to tell me what she's like once you get to know each other."

This was super-great! I couldn't wait to get to Obaachan's, make a new friend, and have more adventures in Hiroshima!

"Are we there yet?" I asked Dad.

He smiled. "Maybe you and Sophie can play cards."

After three rounds of Uno, it was time to eat lunch. Mom had picked up bento boxes at the station before we got on the train. She got me a delicious tonkatsu sandwich. I had only had the fried pork cutlet with the yummy thick sauce on a plate at dinner. I wondered if I could put other dinner foods between bread to make lunch sandwiches. Like spaghetti!

Sophie and I played cards some more and then had reading time. Just when I thought we'd never get there, our train finally arrived in Hiroshima.

We took a taxi from the train station to Obaachan's house. As soon as the taxi stopped, Sophie and I piled out and gazed at the front of a little shop.

Wait a minute . . .

Have you joined Jasmine on all her adventures?
Check out these other stories featuring your favorite brave explorer!